Stories from
Walt Disney's
Fantasia

With illustrations from the motion picture

A Random House Book

The Program

The Pastoral Symphony	Beethoven
The Nutcracker Suite	Tchaikovsky
The Sorcerer's Apprentice	Dukas
Rite of Spring	Stravinsky
Dance of the Hours	Ponchielli
Night on Bald Mountain	Moussorgsky

PRINTED IN THE UNITED STATES OF AMERICA
BY THE WESTERN PRINTING AND LITHOGRAPHING COMPANY

Through the pages of this book you meet the principal players in our picture FANTASIA.

These characters were inspired by the music of great composers but are not necessarily just what Beethoven and the others had in mind.

FANTASIA merely offers one way of interpreting this fine music . . . a way that has seemed exciting to those who created the pictures.

The next time you hear the music from which these stories take their titles, maybe you'll think of Mlle. Upanova and little Hop Low and Pegasus and Mickey and all the rest . . . just as we do.

Walt Disney

Let the pages flip past your thumb . . . fast . . . and see what happens in the lower right corner.

Baby Pegasus

The Pastoral Symphony

Baby Pegasus was a little horse with wings.

He lived with his father and mother and brothers high in the branches of a tree near Mt. Olympus, home of the Greek gods.

One morning, Baby Pegasus woke up feeling very happy. This was going to be an exciting day, for jolly old Bacchus, who tended the vineyard, had invited everyone to a grape festival.

Baby Pegasus wiggled from under his mother's protecting wing and peeked over the edge of the nest.

On the ground far below, he saw a band of unicorns gamboling past. Some frisky fauns skipped gaily alongside them, playing funny little tunes on their pipes. Baby Pegasus knew they were all headed toward the festival.

His father and brothers were already up and flying about, so he eagerly toppled out of the nest, fluttering his little wings frantically.

He didn't fly as well as the others. He hadn't had much

practice yet, but he knew that today he'd have to fly his best so he could keep up with the rest of the family. His mother smiled tenderly at his efforts and flew along near him, ready to help if he got into trouble with his wings.

Away the family soared, through the clouds and over to the vineyard. They settled gracefully on the surface of a lovely pool nearby . . . all but Baby Pegasus, who sat down —plop!—with a big splash.

He heard a giggle and there, laughing at him on the bank, were some beautiful centaurettes who had arrived early for the party. Their handmaidens were waiting on them, braiding flowers into their hair and touching their cheeks and lips with pink berries and petals to make them even prettier than they already were. The centaurettes

Melinda

wanted to look their best, because the centaurs would soon be there.

Even shy Melinda wove a garland of flowers for herself, although she was too bashful to have a special centaur-friend of her own, as the others did.

Half a dozen little cupids flew about, helping wherever they could.

Suddenly one of the cupids spied the centaurs galloping toward the pool. There was a stir of excitement as the girls took quick glances at their reflections to see how they looked. The cupids became busier than ever, twisting a strip of birch bark into a hat for one centaurette, arranging graceful draperies of flowers for another and putting finishing touches on everyone.

The handsome centaurs pranced up and soon each one had found his special centaurette-friend.

All except bashful Brudus, who sat alone and sighed.

When the cupids saw Brudus sitting all by himself and pretty little Melinda sitting all by herself a short distance away, they decided something should be done.

So three of them flew to Melinda and the other three

flew to Brudus. Then, playing a coaxing tune on their pipes, they lured the bashful pair toward each other. It was love at first sight with Melinda and Brudus and as they wandered off together, the cupids smiled knowingly at each other and tactfully flew away.

Just then Bacchus and Jacchus arrived and the fun began. The fauns struck up a rollicking tune while some frolicsome centaurettes danced in a circle around their roly-poly host. Baby Pegasus clambered out of the pool and ran back and forth and all around, kicking up his heels and having the time of his life.

Husky centaurs paraded in, bearing baskets of grapes. They emptied them into the huge vat which Bacchus used for pressing the juice from the fruit. And when the vat was

Bacchus and Jacchus

full, centaurs and centaurettes joined hands in a carefree dance.

Bacchus watched jovially from his seat astride sturdy little Jacchus, but he soon grew tired of just looking on. He wanted to get into the fun himself. So he chose a pretty centaurette for a partner and joined in the dance. Poor Bacchus! His heart was light but his feet were not . . . and in the midst of the gay whirl, he tripped and fell with a thud.

He was such a good-natured old fellow, though, that he just sat on the ground and laughed as heartily as everyone else.

Vulcan

Zeus

But suddenly, in the middle of the laughter, the sky darkened and it started to rain! Quickly everyone scampered for shelter.

From the center of a big black cloud, Zeus, most important of the gods, leaned out and watched them run. Behind him, Vulcan, blacksmith of the gods, was forging giant thunderbolts. As fast as he finished one, he threw it to Zeus,

who hurled it downward, roaring with laughter as everyone dodged.

Bacchus and Jacchus scrambled to safety, falling all over each other in their haste. Father Pegasus raced around, herding his family into a good safe place. Baby Pegasus snuggled under his mother's wing until he could hardly be

seen. Fauns and cupids and unicorns and centaurs and centaurettes all huddled together in the caves nearby.

The storm grew worse. The rain came down in sheets.
The gods of the wind blew their hardest.

But Zeus began to tire of the sport. He decided to roll
up in a billowy cloud and take a nap. There was only one

Apollo

thunderbolt left so when Zeus shut his eyes, Vulcan tossed it down . . . and the storm was over.

One by one Bacchus and his guests ventured out from their hiding places. They watched beautiful Iris, goddess of the rainbow, fly across the late afternoon sky, leaving a trail of colors behind her.

Apollo waved farewell to them as he drove his fiery chariot toward the horizon. Morpheus, clad in his deep blue cloak of night, floated above them.

Regretfully the merrymakers realized that the festival was over and it was time to go home. As the Pegasus family flew back to their nest in the tree, Diana, the moon goddess, shot a comet from her bow, the crescent moon, studding the sky with a spray of glittering stars.

Baby Pegasus smiled drowsily at his mother as she tucked him into the nest for the night. As he closed his tired eyes, he thought blissfully of all the things he'd seen . . . of all the fun he'd had.

He wished that Bacchus would have a grape festival every day in the year!

Dewdrop Fairies

The Nutcracker Suite

One Spring a band of busy fairies was hard at work on the hill. They were too tiny to be noticed but they had very important duties to perform. It was their business to decorate everything in sight with drops of dew.

They flew from one blossom to another, dipping and darting back and forth until every flower, from the proud morning glory to the modest dandelion, sparkled in the early sunshine.

Hop Low

One of the Dewdrop fairies discovered a spider web stretched across the leaves. Quickly she flashed over to it and, with a sweep of her wand, covered the silken strands with shimmering drops. A gentle Spring breeze shook the web playfully and some of the dewdrops rolled down and fell into an upturned flower below.

They splashed on the head of a lazy fairy who was hidden away in that very blossom, taking a nap!

The lazy one peeked out over the edge of the petals sleepily as the other fairies all laughed at her. She shook the dewdrops from her head and sheepishly returned to her neglected work. Still half asleep, she flew against one of the others and as they touched, a shower of fairy dust sprinkled down upon some mushrooms, huddled in a cluster on the ground. They looked like a group of plump little Chinese

in long robes and coolie hats.

When the fairy dust touched them, they swayed back and forth and then jumped up and down. And the next moment, they formed a circle and began a gay dance!

All except little Hop Low, the smallest one, who ran around the outside of the ring, looking for a chance to break in.

The others didn't pay a bit of attention to him, though. They just danced around in a circle. Then they formed two lines and paraded back and forth. Then they leaped up and down, one after another.

But when they jumped up, little Hop Low squatted to the ground. When they bent almost double in deep bows, he capered between them. And when they all turned to the left, he turned to the right. Try as he would, he just couldn't seem to do what the rest were doing but he was having a fine

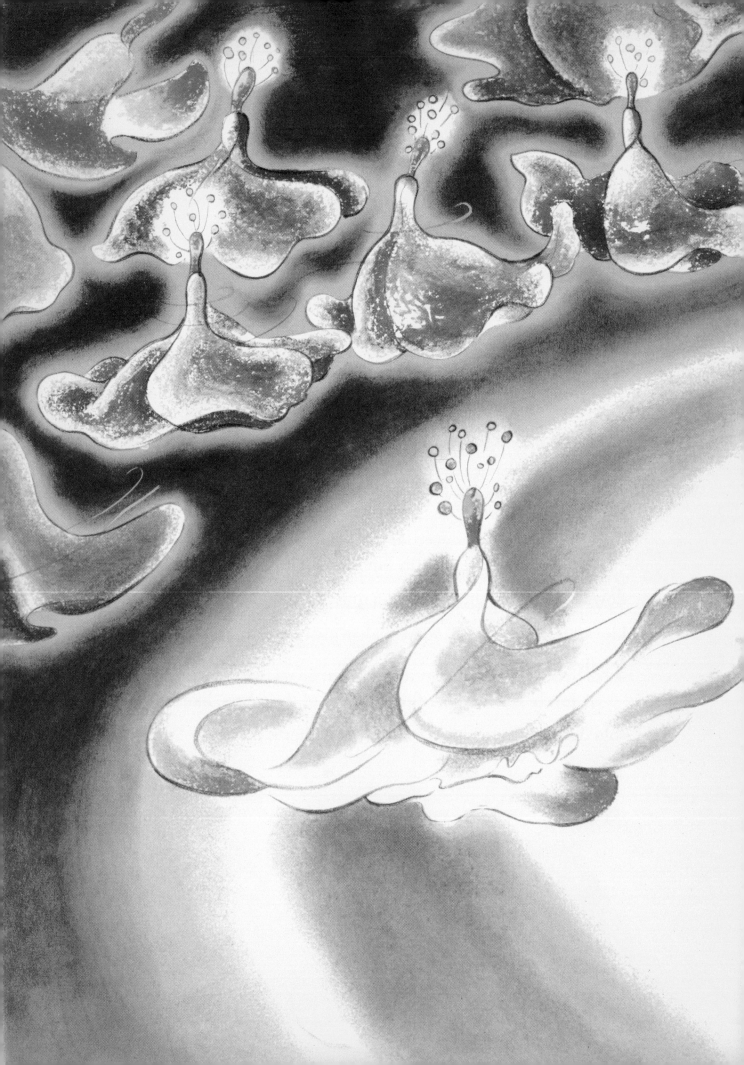

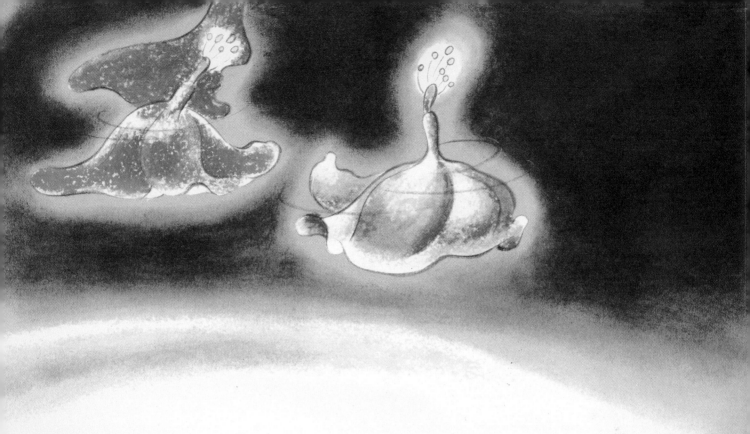

time by himself anyway, spinning 'round and 'round in the sunshine.

As they danced, a warm Summer breeze tossed some flower petals past them toward a quiet stream nearby. The blossoms settled on the water and swirled in slow, graceful spirals and patterns.

A lovely white flower floated ahead of the others, like a solo dancer accompanied by a colorful chorus.

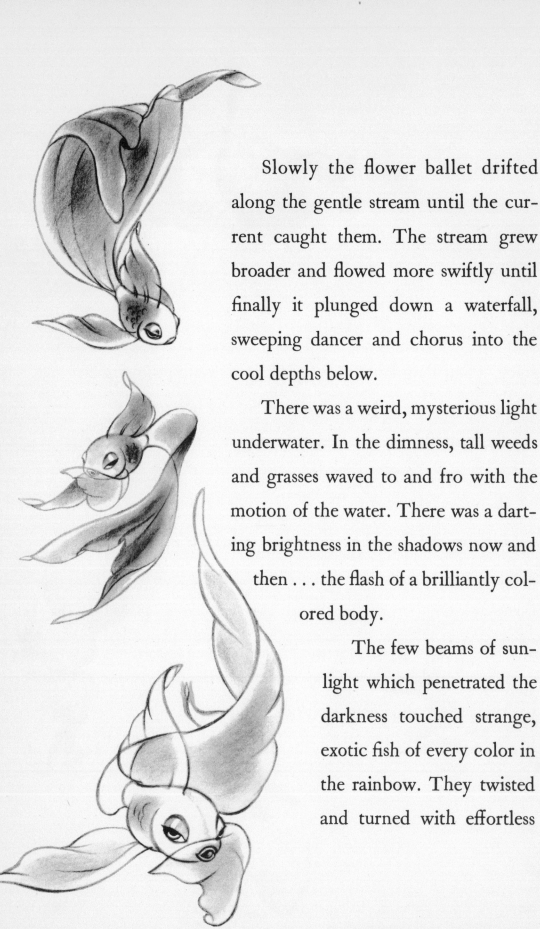

Slowly the flower ballet drifted along the gentle stream until the current caught them. The stream grew broader and flowed more swiftly until finally it plunged down a waterfall, sweeping dancer and chorus into the cool depths below.

There was a weird, mysterious light underwater. In the dimness, tall weeds and grasses waved to and fro with the motion of the water. There was a darting brightness in the shadows now and then . . . the flash of a brilliantly colored body.

The few beams of sunlight which penetrated the darkness touched strange, exotic fish of every color in the rainbow. They twisted and turned with effortless

grace. Their long fantails fluttered in the water, sometimes hiding their faces and veiling them like shy harem girls.

Trails of bubbles marked their paths . . . then rose to the surface.

On the bank of the stream, a clump of thistles nodded their shaggy heads before the wind and a few orchid blos-

Autumn Fairie

soms stirred on the ground behind them, forming a swaying mass of purple in the grass. As the sultry wind blew stronger, the thistles became a band of Russians, whirling and plunging and spinning violently in one of their native dances.

Then it seemed that gay Russian girls in bright orchid peasant costumes twirled forward and joined in the dance. Faster and faster they spun and leaped but when the wind died down, there was again only a clump of thistles and a few orchid petals on the bank.

There seemed to be a new sharpness in the air. The lazy Summer wind was gone and in its place, a crisp breeze heralded the approach of Fall.

In the branches of the willow trees bordering the stream,

Frost Fairies

Autumn fairies now circled busily about, touching the leaves with their magic wands and turning them from green to vivid orange and brilliant red and rich brown. Some of the leaves drifted to the ground, twisting in the brisk wind.

Another band of Autumn fairies opened the milkweed pods. The seeds rushed out like a troupe of ballet dancers, happy to be released.

The wind grew sharper and colder.

The Frost fairies, who always follow close on the heels of the Autumn fairies, soon appeared, sliding gaily down the stems of the plants and flowers and leaving lacy patterns of white on everything they touched. They pirouetted on the water like fancy skaters and in their wake, they left feathery designs of ice.

Then, dancing on the biting wind, the Snowflake fairies appeared, filling the air with eddying crystals of sparkling beauty. They romped over the ground, covering the flowers and plants with a soft white blanket that would keep them snug and warm until the gentle Spring wind returned again to wake them from their Winter sleep.

The Sorcerer

The Sorcerer's Apprentice

Once there was a powerful sorcerer who knew everything there was to know about magic. He lived in an underground cavern with his little apprentice, Mickey Mouse.

Mickey did all the housework . . . and he was getting very, very tired of making beds and cooking meals and running errands and chopping wood and things like that. He wanted to be a sorcerer himself and have an apprentice of his own!

One day the sorcerer was practising some magic. He waved his hands over a bottle on the table before him and instantly a cloud of smoke poured out. It hung in the air a moment and then turned into a beautiful butterfly.

Mickey watched enviously. *That* was the kind of work he wanted to do. But instead, he had to carry water all morning to fill the big tub in the middle of the room, because that's what his master had ordered!

As Mickey watched, the sorcerer waved the butterfly back into the bottle. Then he took off his magic hat, placed it carefully on the table, majestically climbed the stairs and went off to visit a neighboring magician.

As soon as he was out of sight, Mickey set the two water buckets down, scurried over to the master's magic hat and

cautiously put it on.

He looked around the room for something to test the hat's magic. There was an old broom leaning against the wall, so, holding his arms out as he had often seen the sorcerer do, Mickey pointed his fingers at it.

The broom quivered.

It jumped away from the wall.

And then, with a funny little wiggle, it waddled over to Mickey!

Mickey was overjoyed. With the magic hat on his head, he felt he was just as good as the sorcerer. Then he had an idea. Why not let the broom do the work!

He ordered the broom to pick up the two buckets . . . and the broom obeyed him. Then away they went, Mickey and the broom, up the stairs and out to the well. Mickey's new servant filled the buckets with water and back they marched, down the stairs and over to the tub, where the

broom emptied the water and started back for more.

Mickey danced around the room gleefully. He capered over to the sorcerer's favorite armchair, sank down into the cushions and put his feet up on the table. He smiled with satisfaction at the steady swish of the broom as it worked. He thought of all the marvelous things he would do, now that he knew how to make magic.

Mickey closed his eyes blissfully. His head nodded . . . and in a few minutes, he was fast asleep.

In his dreams, nothing was impossible for him to perform. He seemed to be standing on the highest cliff in the world. Like a giant chorus, the stars and planets wheeled and danced in obedience to every gesture of Mickey's arms. Far below, the ocean roared and when he beckoned, the very waves rose to his bidding. Higher and higher the waves dashed, until finally one broke over him . . . and he woke up . . . to find himself splashing around in a room full of water.

While he slept, the broom had carried out his orders so faithfully that the tub had overflowed and the room was flooded. Mickey's chair, bobbing around like a canoe, had finally tipped him into the water.

And the broom was still hard at work!

Mickey frantically tried to stop it. He waved his arms wildly in all the gestures he had ever seen the sorcerer use. But none of them had any effect.

Then Mickey grabbed the broom and tried to pull the

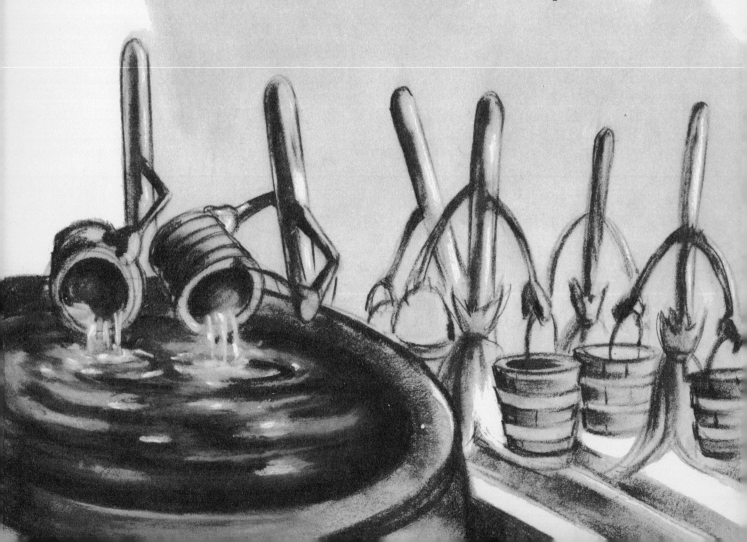

buckets away . . . but the broom was too strong for him.

Suddenly he thought of the axe. *That* would stop it! He dashed up the stairs and over to the woodpile. He snatched up the axe and hid behind the well . . . and when the broom appeared, Mickey was ready for it.

Chop! . . . *Chop!* . . . CHOP! . . . *CHOP!*

He hacked the broom into a hundred splinters. Then he sank down on the top step, exhausted.

Mickey wondered how he would ever get rid of all that water.

Just then he heard a peculiar noise in the courtyard. He

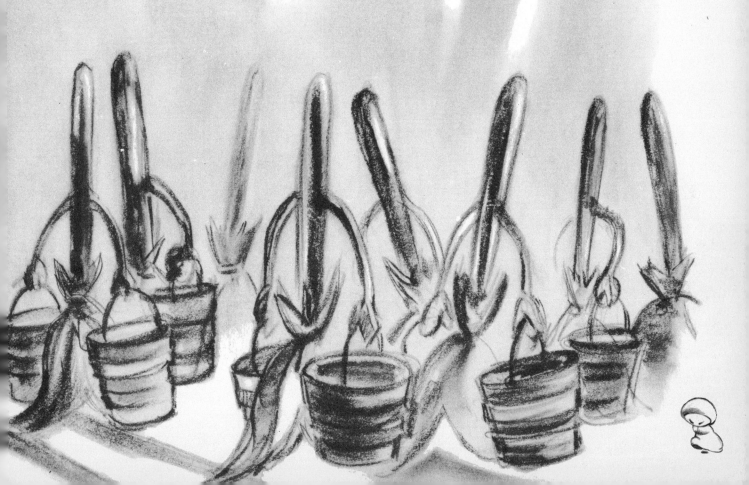

turned around and saw, marching toward him, a whole
army of brooms, each carrying two buckets of water. Every
splinter of the old broom had turned into a new broom . . .
and every new broom was carrying out Mickey's orders!

With a hundred brooms pouring in more and more
water, the room soon became a lake. Mickey saw the sorcerer's book of magic floating around and he dived in after
it. He clung to the pages, desperately looking for the words
that would make everything right again but he just couldn't
find them. Around and around he spun, caught in a whirl-
pool, when suddenly THE SORCERER appeared at the
top of the stairs.

With one piercing glance, Mickey's master took in every detail of the situation. Then he lifted his arms in a commanding gesture . . . and instantly, everything was just as it had been before Mickey put on that magic hat.

The sorcerer walked slowly down the stairs, his gaze fixed on his little apprentice.

Mickey trembled.

Then he remembered he was still wearing the magic hat. He took it off and offered it to his master with a timid little smile. The master snatched it but he didn't smile back at Mickey. He just LOOKED.

Mickey sheepishly picked up the buckets and started toward the stairs.

And as he passed, the sorcerer sped him on his way with a quick spank of the broom, right where it would do the most good.

Stego

Rite of Spring

Millions and millions of years ago, right where you're living now, fierce, ugly beasts roamed the earth. They were so big the ground shook when they walked. They were so strong they could knock over trees just by bumping into them.

Stego was one of the fiercest looking. He was more than twice as big as an elephant and he wore a heavy coat of scales which was almost like a suit of armor. If some other beast started a fight, Stego could usually finish it with just one sweep of his powerful tail.

Diplodocus

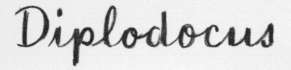

But although Stego was terrible to look at, he was really a peaceful creature at heart and wanted only to be left alone. He didn't have much of a brain. His idea of contentment was to be able to browse among the giant ferns and plants in the jungle clearing until he could eat no more . . . and then to sleep and sleep and sleep until it was time to eat again.

Tritops was Stego's neighbor in the clearing. He had three long sharp horns growing out of his head, and his jaws were so powerful that he could snap a thick tree between his teeth as easily as you would a stick of candy.

Diplodocus lived in the clearing too but he ate his dinner from the treetops. He would stretch his long neck up

Tritops

and around the branches, grab a mouthful of leaves and gulp them down without even chewing. He was so big and his mouth was so small that he had to eat all the time to keep himself alive.

Lazy Bronto spent all his time in the marshy pond beside the clearing. The pond was full of reeds and leaves and mosses that tasted so good to him that he stayed in the water and just ate all day long. He was bigger than a house but he didn't know any more than a three weeks old kitten.

One day Stego and Diplodocus and Bronto and Tritops

Bronto

were placidly munching away as usual when suddenly Tritops lifted his head uneasily. There had been a rumble of thunder in the distance but that wasn't what had roused him. He had heard something else . . . a crashing in the jungle . . . a sound that meant danger.

Diplodocus raised his sluggish head on his snake-like neck and peered restlessly over the treetops. Some gigantic thing was coming toward them, beating its way through the heavy jungle growth.

Only slow-witted Stego kept on eating. He alone didn't seem to realize the danger.

Frightened, Bronto backed into the deepest part of the pond as quickly as he could move his immense body.

With a shudder, Tritops stumbled away. Diplodocus lumbered after him. There was another rumble of thunder. Livid streaks of lightning slashed across the sky. The rain came down in sudden torrents.

All around the clearing, terrified creatures were crashing past into the safety of the black depths of the jungle. Above the noise of the storm, they could hear the unknown monster drawing closer and closer.

And then Stego's jaws stopped their incessant chewing. He had finally become aware of the approaching danger.

His tiny brain thought only of escape. He looked around helplessly, then began a slow retreat, backing away from the oncoming terror. But he was too late. The monster had smashed his way into the clearing. There he stood . . .

REX, KING OF THE TYRANT BEASTS,

the most ferocious and treacherous of all the inhabitants of that brutal world.

With a triumphant bellow, his strong cruel jaws bared

in a snarl, revealing saber-like teeth. His mean, red eyes burned with rage.

Stego stood motionless for a long moment. Retreat was useless. His only chance was to fight. He lashed out violently with that wicked tail.

The lightning flashed and the thunder rolled. Hour after hour the battle raged. The earth trembled with the struggles of the two beasts and the whole jungle rang with their angry roars.

But big and powerful and dangerous as Stego was, Rex was bigger and more powerful and more dangerous . . . and he had only one thought . . . to destroy Stego. With every

Rex

mighty blow and with every vicious lunge, Rex gained ground . . . and Stego's doom became more certain.

When the fight was finally over and Stego's torn body lay lifeless, the victor raised his head in a howl of exultation and triumph.

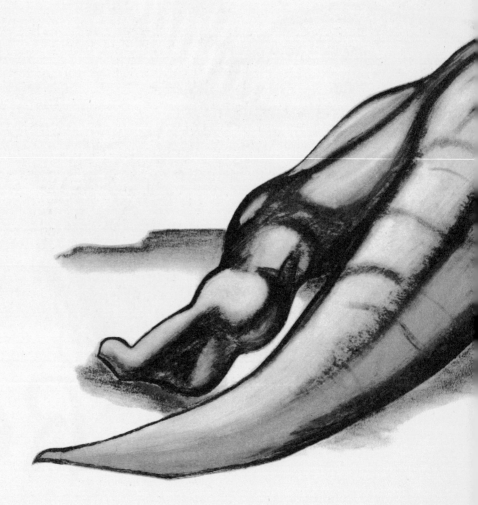

His time would come too . . . and soon . . . but he didn't know that. He knew only that he was once more victorious . . . that he was still

REX, KING OF THE TYRANT BEASTS.

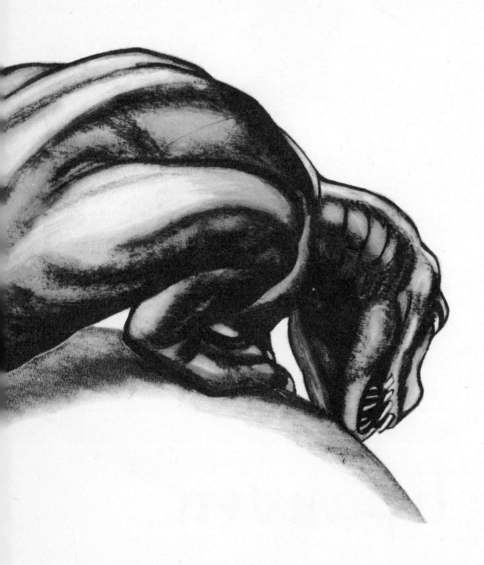

Mlle. Upanova

Dance of the Hours

The beautiful ballroom of the palace was crowded with dancers, all dressed in lovely costumes of gossamer and lace and all eager for the dance recital to begin. They limbered their muscles with graceful little practise steps as they awaited their cues.

Finally the orchestra played the opening chords. A hush fell over the audience as the heavy curtains parted.

Mlle. Upanova, solo ballerina, stood revealed in all her beauty, poised lightly on her toes. In the background, there was a broad stairway and nestled gracefully on every step was a pretty dancer, fast asleep.

With a series of dainty little taps, Mlle. Upanova wakened the dancers one by one, until she was surrounded by the entire ballet chorus. She posed motionless on her toes as the others spiraled around her. Then she leaped into the air.

Once . . . twice . . . thrice . . . but on the third leap, she slipped as she landed. She recovered her balance very

quickly, but naturally she was embar-
rassed. However, little accidents like that
will happen even to such artists as Mlle.
Upanova, so, just as though nothing had
gone amiss, she picked up a cornucopia
filled with fruit, and tossed grapes and bananas and oranges
at the members of the chorus. The ballet girls caught the
fruit with careless grace, never missing a step nor causing a
break in the lovely design of their dance pattern.

Then, like a wave breaking on the shore, they all pirouetted past the classic marble pool in the center of the ballroom and danced out of sight.

Emerging coyly from
the center of the pool was
Hyacinth Hippo. She was a
very vain creature and spent
most of her time admiring
her reflection in the water.

Hyacinth

When her friends ran in, anxious to go into their dance, she insisted that they all help her get ready before she'd dance a step!

So one brought her ballet costume, another brought powder and a huge puff and still another held a mirror while Hyacinth primped. Finally she felt she was beautiful enough and they started their dance.

Each one tried to outdo the others but no one could compete with Hyacinth. She was without question the star and every motion she made, from her fluttering arms to her daintily-pointed toes, proved her superior grace.

They went swaying and spinning all around the great hall until Hyacinth sank down on a divan in a state of complete exhaustion. Her friends quietly withdrew and left her to rest.

Then came the Elephant Girls, who were always more than eager to perform. They frolicked in, tossing bubbles with light-hearted abandon until the air was filled with them. Then a gust of wind carried the bubbles off and the troupe ran out after them.

Hyacinth slept peacefully through it all.

Then, from behind one of the big pillars, a mysterious form crept forward.

Ben Ali Gator, sleek, suave leader of a villainous-looking band, was watching Hyacinth. From behind every pillar, a member of his crew peeked out and watched her too.

With a dominating gesture, Ben Ali ordered the others to withdraw, while he, sweeping his long black cape about his shoulders, approached the sleeping beauty.

He stood beside the divan and looked at her, a wicked leer on his face. Hyacinth stirred restlessly and then opened

Ben Ali Gator

her eyes. When she saw the sinister intruder she gave a frightened start, then jumped from the couch in an attempt to escape his clutches.

But Ben Ali was too quick for her. He seized her . . . as the rest of his murderous-looking followers came spinning in.

It was the introduction of their adagio dance, with Hyacinth Hippo and Ben Ali Gator as the stars!

Theirs was a wild, mad dance. The chorus leaped and bounded while Ben Ali swung Hyacinth over his shoulder with

powerful grace or lifted her triumphantly above his head.

Then, one by one, Mlle. Upanova and her chorus, the Hippo ballet and the Elephant Girls returned to the scene until the entire ensemble was back in the ballroom, twirling in a whirlwind finale.

It was a fitting conclusion to the most spectacular dance recital in history.

Night on Bald Mountain

It was midnight.

The moon shone down on a sleeping village which nestled in a peaceful little valley. Behind the rows of happy homes, the mountain was silhouetted against the moonlit sky like some majestic sentinel standing watch.

As a wandering cloud passed over the face of the moon, strange shadows were cast on the mountain. The peak seemed to be changing shape in a mysterious manner. It was growing taller . . . spreading out . . . stretching upward . . . like a huge bat slowly unfolding its wings.

Then suddenly, with a triumphant gesture of defiance, Satan, Demon of Evil, stood revealed on the mountain top. This was his night . . . Hallowe'en . . . the night when evil held sway . . . the one night in the year when he was able to rise from his den deep in the rocky caverns of the mountain and call to his side all the bad creatures of the world.

Satan stretched his mighty arms and wings . . . and everywhere the shadow of his clawed hands fell, wicked beings rose from the earth and started toward their master. Satan's features twisted in horrible laughter as he watched the ghostly horde approaching him.

Bony white skeletons danced along beside shapeless
trolls and imps; witches on brooms whisked through the
air; a hideous toad perched on the shoulder of a hairy beast.
Goblins and hobgoblins, bogies and banshees, specters

and spooks, black cats and buzzards, phantoms of every kind . . . all joined the awful procession sweeping up and around the mountain.

Satan scooped them into the palm of one huge hand and

there, in the flickering flames, they joined in a wild dance while he gloated over them.

Hour after hour the revelry continued. Satan threw back his head and laughed fiendishly at the weird antics of his subjects. The shrieks and screams of the dancers sounded like the wind howling around the rocks on a stormy night. On and on they danced.

Suddenly, in the midst of the mad frolic, a silvery chime rang out.

The village church bells were pealing out to wake the sleeping villagers as the first faint warning of the approaching dawn streaked across the sky.

Satan cringed in abject fear. The reverent tones of the church bells, symbolic of everything good in the world, meant the end of his power.

The dancers cowered, knowing full well that the light of day quickly overcomes the terrors of the night.

One by one the wraiths of the darkness forsook their master and began slinking back to their resting places in the earth.

Satan buried his head in his arms in a desperate effort to shield his ears from the bells . . . and to shield his eyes from the dawn. He sank deeper and deeper into the mountain.

The sky grew lighter and brighter and when day came and the little village began to stir itself, the mountain top again presented its normal, majestic appearance.

Satan's reign was ended for another year.